SSIT Reports on the Different Breeds of Werewolf, Separate Species of Vampire and Human/Animal Shape Shifters

By Elisha Worthall and Dr. Xavier Bell

ISBN: 978-0-646-56328-2

Circulate Series by K.R. Smith

'Circulate' 1st ed. copyright © 2005

Contents

~~~~~~

FOREWORD

These are the classified reports made by the Circulator Elisha Worthall and the human Dr. Xavier Bell, who run the Supernatural Scientific Investigative Team (SSIT). What began as a recreational club at Cambridge University expanded into a profession. The case files are stored on the Circulate Mainframe, protected behind passwords created by the Circulate Council. Lead Councillor Lucas Hodge used the 21st century multinational corporation Hodge Endeavour, to sponsor SSIT before World War Three halted the investigations.

~~~~~~

SSIT Report On
The Different Breeds Of Werewolf

INTRODUCTION

The following report by the Supernatural Scientific Investigative Team is an analysis of the different breeds of Werewolves in the world.

Unlike Vampires, whose species can be found in most countries, Werewolves are localized to certain continents. No breeds were found in Africa, Australia or South America because other Shape Shifters or paranormal predators claim the African and South American region. Whereas with Australia, it is believed but not yet verified that before the continents divided after the Gondwanaland period, Werewolf migration had not spread that far.

From Elisha Worthall utilizing the Circulate's 25th Century technology, she was able to see back into the Mesozoic era. The Circulator worked in conjunction with her Calculator Patrick O'Flannigan, to track the history of the 'First Werewolf' by homing in on the Werewolf's DNA.

It is now documented that the First Werewolf was a hot-blooded creature, with teeth and claws similar to the Raptor. In fact, the Raptor was the most closely related to this creature in physical characteristics, but it fell short in height and surprisingly, in temperament. Indeed, the only predator that was game to hunt the First Werewolf was the largest of all carnivores, the T-Rex.

If the First Werewolf's prey survived an attack, they would begin to develop many of the First Werewolf's physical characteristics. This was from the dominant Shape Shifter DNA present in the First Werewolf's saliva. The prey in turn, would spread these characteristics when they hunted. Even previous herbivores would turn into carnivores from their mutation. Thus, the Werewolf DNA was spread with each new breed of Werewolf developing.

When the meteor impacted and dust blanketed Earth in an icy darkness, the First Werewolf's 'followers' managed to survive by going into hibernation. Then, as life on the surface of the planet changed, so did its mutated followers. To prevent itself from becoming extinct, the changed prey bred with another species that was the closest that came to a genetic cousin; an early form of the Canidae family. From this coupling, its offspring came to feature more canine aspects.

The First Werewolf's offspring lost it's hard, protective, reptilian-like scales that covered its skin, but its superior strength remained. It also began to decrease in size, with each new mutation through the eons. Today, the breed that most resembles the First Werewolf is the European Werewolf. The size, strength and temperament of this monster today, is in direct hereditary descent from its prehistoric forefather.

Werewolves are man-eaters, attributing their longevity from the bloodlust demanding fresh kill. The only exception to this rule is the Lokoti Werewolf, who started out hunting human, but for the safety of the humans in the Lokoti Tribe, they were able to curb their bloodlust towards animal. Interestingly, the Lokoti Werewolf is the only breed that is not directly descended from the First Werewolf. Similar to animal-spirit possession in other Shape Shifters in Africa; the Lokoti Tribe's history indicates that they were created from both the sharing of blood and spirit between a Lokoti Wolf - a rare subspecies of Grey Wolf in Alaska - and a human tribal member.

With all breeds of Werewolf, four commonalities can be found:
- Allergy to silver; all species of Werewolves like Vampires and other Shape Shifters, are allergic to this metal. They can be killed by either a silver bullet to the heart and brain, or a silver sword through the heart.
- The change when a Werewolf shifts its shape from human to beast.
- The bloodlust which is the controlling urge to feast on fresh flesh.
- The impact of the full moon on the bloodlust, which can trigger a Werewolf to shape shift.

Scanning the cellular structure of several species of Vampire and breeds of Werewolf, it became apparent that both are Shape Shifters. They are able to alter their physical form to hunt or when engaged in combat. The basic 'fight or flight' instinct appears to be the trigger, which engages a Shape Shifter's change. However, a Werewolf shifts their shape the most, particularly the Asian Werewolf.

After further years of extensive study and travelling, we came to realize that similar to human beings, Werewolves also had different physical characteristics. Just as with natural species, supernatural creatures also adapt differently depending on their environment. Some Werewolves were susceptive to meeting us under the strictest understanding that their names would be excluded and the reports would be made confidential. Others, particularly the more dangerous of the breeds, were studied under subterfuge.

Due to the predatory nature of the European Werewolf, when we filmed this breed changing, this was done covertly by Elisha Worthall acting alone. Since European Werewolves are man-eaters, Elisha Worthall was able to use her Circulator ability to instantaneously phase out of danger as soon as the Werewolf picked up her scent. Those who were open to our research were the Lokoti Werewolf pack and one of the Asian Werewolves, from the Hsu Clan.

For a tentative first meeting, Elisha Worthall met three members of the Lokoti Werewolf pack, who were on the Council of Lokoti Tribal Elders. An exchange of information was initiated; in return for SSIT investigating the Lokoti Werewolf, the tribe was permitted to learn about Elisha Worthall's ability as a Circulator. She was instantly recognized as such, whom the Lokoti call 'The Light People'.

A productive union was formed between SSIT and the tribe, as we shared our notes on the four breeds; Lokoti, Asian, European and North American Werewolves. It was from the Lokoti that my associate learned something new about herself; she was informed that Circulators have auras, which can be seen by Werewolves. In fact, we learned that Werewolves could also see a psychic's aura, as can other Shape Shifters such as Vampires.

The Lokoti Werewolves are highly respected by the human members of the tribe, and the secrecy of who was a Werewolf is closely guarded. Indeed, secrecy as Werewolves was a common theme in all of the breeds that were investigated. Just as human murderers must hide their crimes from society to avoid punishment; the Werewolves must hide their supernatural identities to ensure their feeding and therefore survival. This became apparent in every breed but the Lokoti Werewolves, who continue to hunt and feed on human.

LOKOTI WEREWOLF

~Physical Characteristics~

This breed appears the most 'human' in supernatural form, because they maintain their humanoid shape.

When a Lokoti Werewolf shape shifts from human to other, their muscles expand in size as their strength increases by fifty fold. Their eyes glow a different colour, e.g. brown eyes turn blue or yellow. No member of the pack has the same coloured glowing eyes and indeed, a colour can be passed down to the next in genealogy. In their supernatural state, their sight can take on infrared qualities to assist in hunting. Their hand and toenails increase in size and thickness, to become claw-like, as their teeth become elongated and sharper; in particular their canine teeth.

This breed of Werewolf is always male, with fifteen in the pack - no more and no less. When a pack member dies, a human male from the tribe is 'activated', going through the change on the next full moon. It has become evident that the Lokoti Werewolf gene is inherited in all males of the tribe. The age a new Lokoti Werewolf is activated, is typically between 10 - 25 years old.

They have lightening fast reflexes, and can run up to speeds of 200 km/h. Lokoti Werewolves have a keen sense of smell and can track quarry up to 100 km's away. After tasting the blood of their mate, they can track their female's scent over large distances, sometimes up to thousands of kilometres.

The Lokoti Werewolf pack is empathic and can communicate with its members by ESP. Although this breed isn't as skilled as telepaths, they can send out short commands to one another. They empathically sense when another of the pack is in trouble and the same when they take a human female for a mate. They become attuned to the other members and their mate, by feeling their emotions.

This breed no longer hunts human. They successfully placate their bloodlust with animal flesh. Every full moon, the pack hunts together to chase down their quarry on foot, and attack using their claws and elongated teeth. Lokoti Werewolves hunt large game in Alaska, such as caribou, moose, grizzly, black bear, Dall sheep etc. However, they are so attuned to their environment, they can sense when numbers are low and move on to hunt other quarry.

On this note, they are tied to their hunting grounds, so much so they can wane if they are away for long periods of time. They will also wane if they're separated from their pack or mate. When this occurs, the first sign is they can lose control of the bloodlust, although never turning on family or a human in the tribe. Their protective instinct even dominates their murderous inclinations. The second sign is severe depression where the Lokoti Werewolf may lose their will to live and die in their sleep, even if they're not elderly.

However, they have an unusually long lifespan, which can reach up to 200 years. They do not become elderly until surpassing their hundredth birthday. But even in old age, they retain their supernatural strength when they shape shift from human to other. This is due to the bloodlust, as they continue to hunt every full moon, until death.

This breed is supernaturally fast healers; however, like all Werewolves, they are severely allergic to silver. When a Lokoti Werewolf is wounded, another member of the pack will share their blood to aid in their regeneration. This breed can recover from most injuries, although not all. In supernatural form, if one is shot in the head and heart by a normal bullet, there is a fifty percent chance that they will recover. However, if one was riddled with a multitude of bullets, they can die.

~History~

The Lokoti Werewolf has always lived in a particular geographic location, the Lokoti National Park in the Alaska Range. It's situated 4.5 hours north of Anchorage and 1.5 hours south of

Fairbanks. The Lokoti is the only breed of Werewolf that is genetically tied to land. The story of how the first Lokoti Werewolf was created is part of the history of the tribe as a whole.

According to the Tribal Elders, the Lokoti Wolf shared his blood with Aru as the warrior lay dying. The human was grievously wounded after trying to defend his people from an invading tribe that came to take their land and women. It's said to have been a great battle where only fifteen of the warriors survived.

In the legend, the Lokoti Wolf smelled that Aru had a noble spirit and saw he was dying because of defending his mate, young and territory. Since the Lokoti Wolf mates for life, it recognized similar behaviour in the dying human. The old wolf gave his blood, as he gave up his life, so the wounded warrior could live. His spirit also merged with the human, and as the light faded from the wolf's blue eyes, Aru's brown eyes began to glow blue. From this merging, Aru arose as the first Lokoti Werewolf and shared his blood with the fourteen other injured tribesmen. Henceforth, it created the fifteen members of the pack and altogether they drove out the invaders and rescued their families.

According to three members of the pack who sit on the council of Tribal Elders, no Lokoti Werewolf has partaken in human flesh for two centuries. The story of the last time this breed ate human happened in July 1777 AD, during the U.S. War of Independence. What is known of the event, the Lokoti Werewolves attacked a party of English Soldiers, in retribution for the kidnapping and rape of six of their women. The Werewolves killed between 60 - 70 English Soldiers in a brutal attack which did not spare a single soldier's life. Then the Werewolves returned the women to their tribe.

When another party of English Soldiers found the massacre days later, wild animals were blamed for the attack. Due to the fact that none survived, with the appearance of the unused muskets and rifles, it was viewed that the attack had been so sudden that the soldiers were unable to get a shot off in defence. It was because of the magnitude of the violence, the Lokoti Tribal Lands were deemed unsafe for European Settlement for many years.

Then the tribe had little contact with the English, French, Russian or Colonial Americans for another hundred years. That was until Russian Trappers and Colonial Americans, settled in the region next to tribal lands, which eventually became the small township of Alma.

~Reproduction/Mating Habits~

As previously mentioned, the Lokoti Werewolves have, at any one time, fifteen in the pack. The gene is passed along the bloodline from father to son. In cases where there is more than one male child, the gene is activated in the eldest. However, there have been instances in the advent of death of the eldest, can trigger a change in the next male child. This signals that the Lokoti Werewolf gene is present but dormant in the entire male lineage.

When a Lokoti Werewolf reproduces, the tribe call it 'mating'. This process has been described when the Werewolf procreates with a woman, he claims her as his 'mate'. The sexual act has not only the reproductive fluids passing from the male to the female, but the Werewolf also ingests some of the blood of the woman. By doing so, he gains her scent, enabling him to track her up to distances as great as thousands of kilometres away.

The process also hints at some level of empathic as well as biological bonding, as there have been incidents reported where the Werewolf is able to sense if his mate is in trouble and runs to her location, by tracking her scent. Other cases show the biological asymmetry of his genetic qualities, such as strength and regeneration, also developing in the woman.

The reproductive fluids and even the pheromones to lure a mate are potent, with a high fertility rate. There has never been a case where a mating has not produced at least one child, and a male child at that. However, it has also been proven that they are able to control how many children it produces. If the Werewolf senses pregnancy may harm their mate, their bodies decrease sperm production. It's said that the first years of the mating process are the most fertile for the Werewolf, and afterwards it can choose to stop reproducing.

The mating process is for life with the partnership only severed by death. However, with the longevity of a Lokoti Werewolf, when his mate dies he does not take another. This behaviour is similar to other canines such as the fox, which mate only the once. There have also been cases where a mate has died, and sometimes the Lokoti Werewolf wanes to such an extent that they too, lose their will to live.

NORTH AMERICAN WEREWOLF

~Physical Characteristics~

The North American Werewolf has the physical appearance of an upright wolf, which walks and runs on its hind legs.

The hands and feet are changed from a human's five fingers and toes to four, with the small finger and toe conjoining. The North American Werewolf is completely covered in a reddish-brown fur, with a narrow snout and tall ears. Their eyes are completely black and although they cannot see infrared, they have night-vision. Their teeth as well as their nails, become elongated and sharp.

This breed doesn't have supernatural speed like the other breeds of Werewolves. However, they have exceptional hearing, detecting the slightest of noise. They are excellent trackers and can smell their quarry up to distances of a hundred kilometres away. Their physical strength increases by fifty fold when they change, like the Lokoti Werewolf. But unlike their supernatural 'brothers', both men and women can change if they are bitten and the female is just as strong as her male counterpart.

The North American Werewolf has the same lifespan as a human. Like other breeds, the full moon triggers their bloodlust and forces them to change. Even if they are elderly, they are still covered in a reddish-brown fur and are supernaturally strong. They are also allergic to silver, but this breed doesn't have the regenerative capabilities like the others do. This means they can be killed by normal bullets, if they were shot through the heart or head.

This species changes involuntarily every full moon and 'black out' during the process. In some cases, humans who change into this breed are not even aware that they are a North American Werewolf. As they have only been sighted during a full moon, it's conjectured they may transform only during this period.

When the moon is full, this breed will hunt human. It's because of this, they are often found living in the country. When they become aware of their supernatural state, they attempt to isolate themselves for the safety of others. However, due to the 'black outs', this attempt turns futile when the bloodlust takes control.

~History~

The North American Werewolf is often a nomad, and prefers to stay away from large towns or cities. They roam all over the United States and Canada and as such, tracking the source of their origin was difficult. It's believed that this breed wandered the American continent up to a thousand years before European settlement. From the oral histories of several Native American tribes, the creature's migration had been noted by their dealings with it.

It's been recently proven using the Circulate's Viewing Room systems that the North American Werewolf originally came from South America. The former 'South' American Werewolf, migrated to new hunting grounds when it encountered a greater predator than itself; mankind. Certain South American tribes induce animal spirits to encourage possession of a human host, temporarily giving the human extra sensory perception or increasing physical prowess. Before European weapons such as muskets were introduced, many South American tribes ritualized war and hunting. Using animal spirit possession, it enabled the humans to battle the 'South' American Werewolf as well as the South American Vampire. As such, it caused a territorial dispute and thus this breed travelled north.

Over the centuries this man-eater attacked many, with some killing the creatures or survivors who found out about their change, the following full moon. Those who were lucky enough to live through an attack were changed by bite, to turn into the monster they thought they destroyed. Upon learning of the blood on their hands after their first change, the new Werewolf went on the run. According to the oral history of one tribe, one group of North American Werewolves 'ran' so far up north, they entered Alaska.

The Lokoti Tribal Elders told SSIT of the time the Lokoti Werewolves battled a band of eight North American Werewolves, in the mid 19th Century. This is the only case that SSIT came upon, of the North American Werewolf existing in a pack. The Elders told that upon their change, the North American Werewolves who were made up of both Colonial Americans and members of differing Native American tribes; had to leave their homes when they became wanted for murder.

It was a night of the full moon when the eight North American Werewolves, stumbled into Lokoti Werewolf territory. The man-eating breed was hunting and attacked the tribe when the pack was away, on its own hunt. However, the Lokoti Werewolves empathically sensed their human mates' distress and returned early. It's said to be a bloody battle, with the North American Werewolf strength an equal match to the Lokoti Werewolf. However, the Lokoti gained the upper hand with their faster reflexes.

The fifteen Lokoti Werewolves decimated the eight North American Werewolves. Then they shared their blood with the injured humans of the tribe. Their blood's regenerative properties helped to heal, as the anti-bodies destroyed the North American Werewolf DNA in the bite marks. This prevented the humans from turning into new North American Werewolves on the next full moon.

This instance also implicates that cross-contamination would not work, if a human was bitten by two separate breeds. The human would either turn into one breed or another, but not have elements of both. This feature sets Werewolf genetics apart from its other Shape Shifter 'cousin', the Vampire. When investigating the separate species of Vampires, SSIT found that the North American Vampire was a hybrid of the South American and the European. However, this is also remarkable of Lokoti Werewolf DNA; that it will not turn humans into their kind, but it can be used to stop a transformation into another breed.

Although the eight North American Werewolves didn't survive to tell the tale, it's interesting to note that this breed never crossed into Alaska again. This hints that their survival instinct navigates them away from another's territory, once an enemy becomes known. The fact that this breed has never returned to the continent of South America, supports this theory. But how this information is relayed, either genetically or by means of ESP, is unknown.

~Reproduction/Mating Habits~

North American Werewolf genes cannot be carried on via means of sexual reproduction. Therefore, a child born to a parent who is a North American Werewolf does not have the genes to turn into this breed. Instead, they multiply by infecting humans with the saliva in their bite. However, due to the dangerous nature of the bloodlust, not many survive an attack and therefore, the numbers created are few.

This breed has never been sighted with a long term mate. It's believed because of their nomadic nature, they are often on the run. The second reason is due to their inability to control the bloodlust during their change. There have been tragic incidents where a person who was a North American Werewolf and not know it, discovered their dangerous nature the morning after. When this occurs, the Werewolf awakens to find their spouse or family's partial remains, with their hands and mouths covered in the victim's blood.

As such, they normally live alone in remote areas as they attempt to avert disaster by isolating themselves.

ASIAN WEREWOLF

~Physical Characteristics~

This breed appears the most like a wolf when it shifts shape.

The body completely changes from an upright, bipedal human appearance, to a four-legged form of a large wolf, with a silvery-grey coat. The fur springs forth from the pores in the skin then retreats back into the body, when they revert. They have white eyes with small black dots, as pupils. In the dark, their eyes appear to be glowing white, by reflecting the light. In their Werewolf form, this breed does have night-vision.

Asian Werewolves walk and run on all fours, with their shoulder and hip bones contorting to adjust to the front and back legs. Indeed in their supernatural form, it's hard to distinguish an Asian Werewolf from a Grey Wolf, except for the white eyes, larger size and their front legs being slightly shorter than their back legs. With such a dramatic shape shift, the Asian Werewolf is the only breed which remains in their supernatural form if they should die as such, whereas the others return to human.

Their strength increases by twenty fold and both males and females, can change into this breed; with females just as strong and as fast as their male counterparts. Although Asian Werewolves are not as strong as the other kinds, they are the fastest, running up to speeds of 400 km/h. They are also the best trackers as their sense of smell is legendary. There are stories of victims being unable to escape a vendetta placed on them, even if they moved to the other side of the world.

The life span of this breed is up to 150 years and even if the Asian Werewolf is elderly, it's still strong and fast in its supernatural form. Like all breeds, the full moon triggers its bloodlust and causes it to shape shift. However, it can also turn without this influence, when it's tracking a target or to engage in combat.

~History~

The Asian Werewolf has been sighted all throughout Asia, predominantly in Mongolia, China, Korea and Japan. However, there are reports of clans so far as Hong Kong, Taiwan, Malaysia and the Philippines. This breed is both nomadic just as it is territorial. Some Asian Werewolves travel extensively, due to the bloodlust making it difficult for them to hunt in one location. With others, and particularly in the case of clans, live in rural areas and have claimed the region for centuries.

Like the European Werewolf, this breed has the most sightings and coincidentally, an extensive history recorded by humanity. The sightings of this species go back to BC – Before Christ. The Asian Werewolf has appeared in literature, as well as artwork in temples and lastly, in ceremonies similar to the Dragon Dance, which is usually performed on Chinese New Year.

In Buddhist temples in China, Korea and Thailand, as well as a Shinto temple in northern Japan; artwork has been sighted depicting enlarged wolves, with silvery-grey coats and glowing white eyes. In one of the ancient ruins inside the jungles of Cambodia, there is a carving on a wall of a past King fighting an enlarged dog-like creature, with claws and teeth like a tiger.

Similar to 'hell money' used for the deceased, there are customs for protection against Asian Werewolves. One such custom in China is to bang cooking utensils during a lunar eclipse, to scare 'the dog of heaven' (1). Small, silver charms tied together with red wool, are strewn over doorways; however, this tradition is not only to protect the inhabitants from Asian Werewolves, but also Asian Vampires. Silver charms also decorate some cribs, due to the fact that pregnant women and infants are said to be an Asian Vampire's source of nourishment. In India, small silver bells on bracelets and anklets are commonplace with a sari, whereas with Feng Shui, silver bells are also used to dispel negative energy in clearing ceremonies. This was also a tactic used to ascertain if a Shape Shifter was darkening your home.

Although the majority are man-eaters, some clans are highly respected in protector-like roles. In rural areas where they have lived for centuries, humans pay them homage. Arrangements exist where humans will not be preyed upon if they keep to an agreement or, a clan will protect a town from stray Werewolves or even from Asian Vampires. An intricate honour system prevails, similar to a social class system, where giving offence could be treated as a death sentence.

On this note, Asian Werewolves are extremely territorial, and wars among the clans are typical. There is one example of where the Hsu and the Hsin Clans, in two neighbouring provinces by the Great Wall of China, have been battling for centuries. The war started when a male Asian Werewolf from the Hsin family, eloped with a female Asian Werewolf from the Hsu Clan. Since the Hsu family didn't bestow their permission on the courtship, the marriage was called a kidnapping; although the bride willingly went to live with her husband and his kin. Ironically, over time with the reduction in female Werewolves in the world, kidnappings have become a reoccurring theme. Sadly though, in these instances, the 'brides' aren't whisked away in romantic circumstances.

Once a vendetta is placed on you and the Asian Werewolf never gives in, it would appear that these two sides will continue to fight until the other is eradicated. When Dr. Xavier Bell asked a member of the Hsu Clan why peace-talks have never been initiated, he inadvertently almost placed a vendetta on himself. Apparently, any talks of ending the dispute would be seen as 'losing face', a high dishonour in this culture. After the doctor apologized profusely for his gross offence, the vendetta was never placed upon him.

~Reproduction/Mating Habits~

When the Asian Werewolf reproduces, its progeny also turns when the child reaches puberty.

This breed can also turn humans into their kind by bite, or sharing blood with the chosen. However, they are cautious over whom they turn, and there is never an accidental turning of a stranger. If an Asian Werewolf bites a human, it is either to kill them, eat them or to change them, in a carefully planned manoeuvre.

Since Asian Werewolves are territorial, this in turn makes them overprotective of their mates and young. This breed is monogamous whilst their mate is alive; however, if they die then they may take another. Those who live in clans can communicate with its members via ESP, which also results in couples becoming empathically attuned to one another. If they sense their mate is in trouble, they run to their aid using their keen sense of smell.

Due to their dangerous natures, if an Asian Werewolf takes a human for a mate, they will attempt to turn them. This is to ensure their survival, so they will not be accidentally eaten in the bloodlust-induced craze. In turn, couples and family units can be seen hunting together, under a full moon.

EUROPEAN WEREWOLF

WARNING: this breed is both the largest and the strongest and coincidentally, the most dangerous.

~Physical Characteristics~

The appearance of a European Werewolf is a giant, hairless beast, part man and part wolf.

When they change from human to other, their height almost doubles and their width triples. Their weight is attributed to their strength, which is increased by a hundred fold and even in human form, its overpowering. Both men and women can turn into this breed; however, females are not as strong or as large as their male counterparts.

They have glowing green eyes, with their circular pupils changing into narrow slits. In Werewolf form, they can see infrared which aids in their hunting. Their hands and feet become claw-like, which are sharp and strong and can cut through metal. Their heads take on canine features with a short, stubby snout over jaws of razor sharp teeth. The colouring of the European Werewolf changes, depending on the hair colour in human form. For a person with blonde hair, their hairless skin becomes a light tanned colour; for a person with brown hair, they become brown all over; for a person with black hair, their hairless skin turns a black colour.

The European Werewolf's sense of smell is almost a match to the Asian Werewolf and they are the second fastest of the species. Although this breed can walk upright, it runs on all-fours and can reach speeds up to 300 km/h. They have the highest body temperature of all the Werewolves, consistently sitting at 43 degrees Celsius, which in a human being would be fatal.

This breed is a man-eater and is capable of changing in between full moon cycles, to hunt human. Because of their large appetites, the bloodlust is the strongest in their kind, which causes them to constantly crave human flesh. Coincidentally, many turn into sociopaths since their dangerous cravings conflict with society's morals.

European Werewolves live the longest, up to 300 years old. With such a longevity they do not become elderly until they reach 250 years. However, since they are extensively hunted by European Vampires, it's seldom they reach old age. European Werewolves are superior healers of all the breeds and are able to regenerate from almost all kinds of injuries. It is for this reason that European Vampires hunt them, to drink their blood and temporarily take on their regenerative capabilities. However, like all Shape Shifters, this breed is severely allergic to silver. The few ways to kill a European Werewolf is decapitation, or to run a silver sword through its heart, or silver bullets through both its heart and its head.

It's postured that one of the reasons why European Werewolves have such a powerful regenerative ability, is because their enemy the European Vampire has poisonous fangs. Their poison will not kill the Werewolf, but it can paralyse the monster for up to seven days. However, European Werewolves can heal each other from poisoning by sharing blood. The ingestion of another's life force strengthens their body's immune system and adds to their own.

~History~

European Werewolves have always been at war with European Vampires. What started as a territorial dispute between the predators, turned into Werewolves becoming the Vampires' prey. Since European Vampires cannot heal without imbibing blood from a living being, what better nourishment than a creature which can heal from almost anything.

European Vampires have the longest lives in the supernatural world, reaching 500 years old. They are also the fastest species of Vampire, as they can move at the speed of sound. However, they are not that strong nor can they heal easily, like other Shape Shifters can. Because of this fact, they turned hunting European Werewolves into somewhat of a 'blood sport'; as animals to feed upon for their strength and regenerative capabilities. But just as hunting can be a dangerous sport in the human world, many a European Vampire has been killed by the monsters it was preying upon.

In the medieval times, a high concentration of European Werewolf numbers were found in mountainous parts of Eastern Europe. This is where recorded battles took place between European Werewolves and European Vampires - as the Vampires fought for dominance and the Werewolves fought for survival. Even today these battles continue, although not in as great as numbers as they occurred then.

Now in the 21st Century, European Werewolves in dwindling numbers are scattered all over the continent, particularly in the northerly regions. With their high body temperatures, they only venture southwards to the Mediterranean in the cooler months of the year. They are nomadic, constantly moving around because of the bloodlust forcing them to continually hunt. With such a dangerous appetite, this man-eater is always running from the law.

This breed has the longest history, being the direct descendant of the First Werewolf. Stories of this monster stretch from early BC to the present AD and are extensive, changing with each new storyteller. There is the legend of 'Cerberus' in Ancient Greek mythology, to Skoll and Hati in Germanic mythology. The large wolves, Skoll or Hati, both born by a giantess, are said to chase the sun or the moon across the sky (2); which resembles European Werewolves in their huge, hulking bodies and of course, their never ending hunger. Or, there are horror stories such as 'Hell Hounds'. Canines with scorching breath and described to come from the depths of hell, could be relegated to a European Werewolf's abnormally high body temperature and glowing eyes.

There are records in several Roman Catholic and Orthodox Church documents, from the European Witch Hunts and onwards, which give examples how this breed may only be killed by silver weapons. The documents disclose cases where humans have made unsuccessful attempts to either burn, drown or decapitate, captured European Werewolves.

In 16th Century Budapest, the Church Inquisitors tried to burn a male European Werewolf by tying it to a stake. However, when it changed, its hardened skin and muscle bulk, coupled with its speedy-regeneration, was able to withstand serious damage from the flames. Once the thick rope which held it captive was burned through, the European Werewolf leapt upon the Church Inquisitors and ate them before the horrified crowd.

In 17th Century Prague, an angry mob tried to drown a female European Werewolf for eating several young children. They chained it to a log and then held it under water. But the female European Werewolf changed into it's stronger and larger shape, breaking the thin chains. Next, it leapt out of the water and ate several more humans, sending the rest running for their lives.

In 18th Century Lyon, a male European Werewolf was arrested after fighting in a tavern, where it ate several people including a barmaid. When it had passed out from excessive drinking, it was dragged to a jail cell to wait execution, which was to take place the next morning. However, just before the law-keepers were able to behead the creature in the guillotine, it woke up. It expanded into its Werewolf shape and the guillotine which was not made of silver, actually bounced off its hardened hide and went flying into the executioner, cutting him in half instead. The European Werewolf ate the leftovers and then bounded off, through the screaming audience.

~Reproduction/Mating Habits~

This breed has never been sighted with a long-term mate, as they prefer to live alone. This is attributed to being extremely territorial during a hunt, as they do not like to share their kill. This puts them in direct contrast to Asian or Lokoti Werewolves, who hunt in packs and share their prey.

With their volatile temperaments, after the medieval wars, they have not been sighted in packs again. This is especially since small arguments can erupt into a fight to the death among their kind. On this note, it's very rare a male or female European Werewolf will mate with each other. If this does occur, the union is short lived when a physical fight ensues and they cease their association.

Unfortunately for humans, it would appear that the European Werewolf lust is as great as its bloodlust. With this breed's overpowering strength, it's extremely hazardous to engage in sexual relations. Also, this breed often loses control of the bloodlust in excitement, and would claw and bite the woman. If a male European Werewolf does have sex with a human woman, she can die from her injuries.

With this said of the male, it could be different in the case of the female. Since female European Werewolves are not as strong or as large as their male counterparts, a human male has a greater chance of surviving a sexual encounter. This is of course providing the female does not lose control of her bloodlust, and claw and bite the man.

If a female European Werewolf is impregnated by a human, the foetus develops as a full Werewolf, proving that even the DNA of this monster is overpowering. As such, European Werewolf children are born immediately as Werewolves. However, throughout the long history of this breed, European Werewolf young are rarely sighted. It's believed because their Werewolf parent loses their temper if the child misbehaves, and destroys their offspring.

With such a dangerous nature, sexual reproduction of this species is limited. Therefore, in the majority of cases, European Werewolves are created by being bitten by another. Humans will also turn if they become infected with this breed's blood. The supernatural DNA changes the human on the next full moon, when the lunar cycle impacts the bloodlust. But because of the size, strength and temperament of this predator, hardly any humans survive an attack. This, as well as being hunted by European Vampires, fortunately keeps numbers low.

CONCLUSION

When SSIT investigated Vampire legends in Eastern Europe, we stumbled across the existence of Werewolves. By studying numerous historical documents and talking to members of the community; our investigators came across stories which linked European Vampires to European Werewolves. After we filmed, scanned and unsuccessfully tried to interview a European Werewolf subject, this led to researching the other breeds.

As previously noted, if a human is cross-contaminated with the DNA of two separate breeds of Werewolf, they will turn into one or the other but not both. On this note, there has never been a case of the differing breeds mating with each other to create a cross-breed. Due to this, there is no scientific evidence to back up or dispute that this would even be possible. Instead, it would appear that whenever they do cross paths, they attempt to destroy each other in violent territorial displays.

However, another commonality the differing breeds have is how their flesh reacts to silver. Although all Shape Shifters are severely allergic to this alloy, Werewolves have the greatest reaction. Not only do they bleed heavily, but a red smoke will appear where their flesh came into contact with it. This indicates a chemical reaction between the flesh and the metal.

It was many years later that SSIT came across another branch in this supernatural family - Human/Animal Shape Shifters. All across the globe in various cultures, there are human beings who are able to morph into an animal of similar size. The histories of how this anomaly has occurred are bountiful; from spirit possession to genetic mutation and even through cross-species reproduction. Although the kinds of animals the humans can turn into is varied, there is a commonality in every single one - the eyes. Whenever a Human/Animal Shape Shifter changes into their supernatural form, their eyes appear completely black.

In India whilst in the jungle, SSIT caught on camera, an adult tiger minding a small human child. Upon zooming in, the investigators noted that the tiger's eyes were unusual by the fact that they were 'blacked out'. Further to the investigator's surprise, the tiger changed the child's diaper and then slung it onto its back, to take it into town. My partner in SSIT Elisha Worthall, was able to follow unnoticed by engaging her ability to instantaneously phase. She later reported how the tiger went through a backdoor of a house, which was on the outskirts of town and then minutes later, a woman walked out the front door carrying the same child. When the woman recognized Elisha Worthall from the jungle, her brown eyes blacked over, as a warning.

Indeed, SSIT discovered the indicator linking Human/Animal Shape Shifters to Werewolves and even to Vampires - is the eyes. The eyes of the North American Werewolf are also completely black, when they shift into their supernatural shape. An Asian Werewolf's white eyes with only the black pupils, is identical to a West African Vampire or similar to a European Vampire's completely white eyes. A member of the Lokoti Werewolf pack has glowing red eyes, whereas the South American Vampire has red eyes. Both Lokoti and European Werewolves eyes glow, and both can see infrared.

What is interesting, as much as the members of the Shape Shifter family are similar; each will refute it vehemently. All three have fought over territory, when protecting their own, or to feed off the other. Cannibalism is rife, particularly in the Vampire species whose parasitic natures rely on absorbing another creature's life force. But instead of making allowances, they try to cancel the other out and claim dominance. Although Human/Animal Shape Shifters do not lust after flesh or blood of the living, the bloodlust is inherent in their absolute abhorrence for their supernatural cousins. This is a shame, considering how similar Werewolves and Human/Animal Shape Shifters really are.

~~~~~~~~~~~~~~~~~~~~~~~~~~~~~~~~~~~~~

SSIT Report On
The Separate Species of Vampires

INTRODUCTION

Of all the legends of Shape Shifters in the world, Vampires have one of the longest and most varied history.

When the Supernatural Scientific Investigative Team began to look into Vampire legends of Eastern Europe, the first species discovered was the European Vampire. Then as the investigation deepened, more and more legends, superstitions and stories based on historical and/or cultural fact of this type of Shape Shifter became known. It became apparent that Vampires differ just as humans around the globe do. However, a common factor arose which indicated Vampires are Shape Shifters - in their transition from human to 'other'.

In the case of the different breeds of Werewolves, their Shape Shifter DNA could be linked to a genetic forefather, 'The First Werewolf', which was a hot-blooded predator located in the Mesozoic Age. As discussed in the introduction of the SSIT Report on the Different Breeds of Werewolves, the 'First Werewolf' had similar physical characteristics to its prehistoric cousins such as the Raptor. However the true origins of Vampire DNA are much harder to track, due to the range of cultural differences such as 'the cause' of becoming a Vampire.

Vampire DNA changes the living body to a state of near death; or scientifically put, Vampires enter a kind of biological 'stasis' which shuts down many of their normal functions. This permanent paralysis of organs may heighten certain physical abilities, but it will also decrease others to the point of necrotizing flesh. Some Vampires change from a human appearance to their other form at will, when engaged in hunting or combat. With other species, undergo a complete transformation that it's sometimes difficult to look human once more.

Interestingly, some Vampires share similar physical traits as Werewolves. Another commonality is the 'bloodlust', which is the overpowering need to drink fresh blood or eat fresh kill. Then of course, there is the allergy to silver, which is apparent in all Shape Shifters.

Many species of Vampire are also allergic to garlic. This is because the unique combination of vitamins, minerals and other chemicals found in this organic product, results in a side effect of thinning the blood. Vampires encounter great difficulty regulating their blood, since many of their internal organs that normally do this in a human body, are either no longer functioning or functioning properly. Due to this, imbibing garlic or any kind of drug or plant, which affects the thickening or the thinning of blood, is detrimental to a species whose health is solely based on the principle of never changing. However, if a Vampire is poisoned by garlic or another plant or drug, they can regenerate by drinking blood.

By imbibing the life force of their chosen prey, it became apparent that they take on many of their victims physical traits. What needs further investigating by SSIT, is that if a European Vampire should feed on a human with ESP; they also develop this paranormal ability. Werewolves as well as Vampires can differentiate a psychic from a non-psychic human, by their differing bio-electromagnetic field, which is also called their aura. It is by honing in on the human with the aura, they hunt psychics for their uncanny talent.

The Vampire's urge to feed on fresh blood or other biological matter is similar to the Werewolf's bloodlust. If a Werewolf should eat 'bad meat' i.e., flesh from a corpse which decomposition had begun, or even if the human is ill; this can affect the health of the creature. It's the same if a human ate meat which was infected by debilitating bacteria such as Salmonella. On this premise, Vampires must feed on fresh blood from a healthy being as it can and does affect their health and therefore their longevity.

Much of the Western world term Vampires as the 'undead', although doubtful to apply in the natural world, one can relegate this term loosely to particular Vampire species. Where some Vampire's organs undergo a change to become stronger, others became damaged and ergo useless. However, Vampires still have a heart rate, pulse and therefore breathe, which enables their bodily movements by transporting the blood to their muscles. But in the change to Vampire, the medical drawbacks are numerous, which in turn is responsible for their need to feed on fresh blood.

Another superstition about Vampires, which needs to be quashed is the notion that they are immortal. This is scientifically impossible due to the fact that not even the universe is immortal. With differing scientific groups such as NASA or otherwise, proving with their work in astronomy or physics on matter, anti-matter, dark matter, atoms and molecules, with The Big Bang as well as The Big Crunch, very little let alone biological matter can be deemed to be 'eternal'.

Many species of Vampire have a supernaturally long existence due to a successful feeding pattern. But what became obvious was that for many, if their feeding pattern was not successful then neither was the longevity of the subject. This can be said for any biological creature in the natural world. If the living conditions are plentiful in providing for the life form, then the life form will flourish. However, if food or other necessary elements to survive are not available, then the life form may either change to adapt to their environmental conditions or perish.

Vampires maintain an ambient body temperature, depending on their environmental conditions. This means that they do not sweat from hot weather nor do they suffer from hypothermia. With this said, Vampires still encounter physical injury from frost bite. Because of this, Vampires are very wary of what they experience as they must be careful not to damage their flesh even if they do not always feel pain.

By their bodies existing in a semi-stasis, they may not age; however, another drawback to this is they encounter a great deal of difficulty in healing from physical injury. Vampires may heal themselves after physical harm by drinking either human or Werewolf blood, with the latter their preferred choice. Because of this, particular species such as the European Vampire, have extensively hunted Werewolves - primarily the European Werewolf. When they drink from this other supernatural creature, they take on their physical attributes such as their greater strength and their powerful regenerative ability for up to seven days.

With this said, the same is applied to Vampires drinking human blood. By drinking from a healthy human then the Vampire is able to replenish its protein, vitamins, minerals, sugar-level, white cell count, red cell count and anti-bodies. However, should the Vampire drink blood from a decomposing body or a human with an illness, this can severely weaken them and in some cases lead to their demise.

Another myth in popular culture of Vampires being allergic to sunlight needs to be re-examined. Since they must be continually hydrated by drinking fresh blood, they are photosensitive to bright light and in particular Ultraviolet rays. Humans encounter sunburn every day and from this exposure, they heal by their skin cells reproducing to replace the damaged ones. But because Vampires do not age, their skin is also in stasis and unable to repair itself. They will not turn to dust from exposure to sunlight, but they cannot heal from sunburn unless they drink blood.

By examining the separate species of Vampire, SSIT barely scratched the surface of this global phenomenon. The subjects in this report, shows just how polymorphic this supernatural creature can be. Each species which was investigated, differed physically by appearance, dietary requirements, longevity and living conditions. Another important note was the different causes of how humans or even other biological life forms could be turned into a 'Vampire'. Due to this, the true origin of 'Vampire' cannot be traced to one pure source.

On a humorous note, from a brush over the subject of Vampirism in Wikipedia, there are people in the Balkans who believe and even documented that they have Vampire Pumpkins and/or Watermelons. The symptoms are trembling, growling and 'blood' appearing on the epidermis of the fruit or vegetable. Apparently there are two ways this fruit and vegetable can become a Vampire. The first - if the fruit or vegetable is left outside on the night of a full moon and the second - if the fruit or vegetable is kept more than 10 days after Christmas (3). The first leans towards Werewolf legends with those affected by the lunar cycle. The second reason crosses into the subject of religion and how Vampires can sometimes be called 'The Damned'.

Religious implications on Vampires are minimal. Religion does not have any scientific effect on this species of Shape Shifter. In this scientist's view, religion is folklore itself and is generally used to either inspire false hope or try to explain the unexplainable; however, my partner on SSIT Elisha Worthall, agrees to disagree on this matter with her ever-present crucifix worn around her neck. Holy water and crucifixes to do not work to ward off the Vampires that SSIT investigated. On this note, Vampires can certainly attack human religious figures as well as freely enter a church, and set foot on sacred or consecrated ground. When SSIT investigated European Vampires for instance, we interviewed many members of the community in different Eastern European countries. We encountered several stories of how humans had escaped a Vampire attack by the use of crucifixes as well as by running into a church.

When we asked the witnesses to show us the crucifixes, we found that they were in jewellery form and made of silver. Then we asked to see the church which the subjects had found safety in, to find the buildings had unkempt cemeteries surrounding them. As the up-keep on the said cemetery was not immaculate, this caused the grass to grow long and flowering weeds to appear. Two of these weeds were not in fact weeds, but upon closer examination there were smatterings of flowering garlic stalks as well as 'Wolf's Bane', Arnica Montana that in certain locations in Europe grows abundantly. 'Wolf's Bane' can be used for human medicinal purposes but if used incorrectly, it can cause severe gastroenteritis and even internal bleeding of the intestinal tract (4). These symptoms can be deadly to Vampires and even injure a Werewolf. With this evidence in mind, SSIT concluded that the European Vampires broke off their pursuits, due to the fact silver or because of the flora which was present, when the humans sought sanctuary.

From examining the differing legends of Vampire, the idea that they can also change into animals such as a bat or a wolf, can be allocated to their cellular structure being members of the Shape Shifter 'family'. However, on this note, when investigating the European Vampire, North American Vampire, South American Vampire and West African Vampire, SSIT did not find any evidence that these Vampires could shift their shapes in such a way. The Vampires that SSIT investigated and gathered factual data and biological evidence, always retained a humanoid form. SSIT did another investigation on Human/Animal Shape Shifters from Africa, India, Asia and the Americas, on beings who were able to completely transform into native animals of similar size.

The example of the 'Vampire Pumpkin or Watermelon', of how a fruit or vegetable may have characteristics of a supernatural creature, goes to show how sometimes the term 'Vampire' can be used to define in psychoanalytical terms the 'other'. This is generally feared as it hovers on the boundaries of the known and the unknown universe. Indeed by investigating the global legends of the Vampire, SSIT encountered stories of when a human was simply born different i.e. were albino or had red hair and this was even called Vampire by some cultures. By allowing fear to breed by simply not being able to understand something, easily results in stories to tell children when you tuck them into bed at night. It is through investigation and collecting facts that the truth can be taught instead.

EUROPEAN VAMPIRE

~Physical Characteristics~

WARNING – This species of Vampire has poisonous fangs which can kill humans.

When a European Vampire changes from human to their supernatural form, their eyes turn completely white and their upper canine teeth become long and sharp like the fangs on a snake. This species of Vampire has venom that is secreted by the fangs which can kill humans and paralyse Werewolves. The nails on the European Vampire's hands can become longer and sharper, although not as strong as claws on other supernatural beings. This means they can pierce human tissue; however, they may break on harder substances like clothing such as denim or leather.

The strength of a European Vampire is ten times that of a human. They have supernaturally fast reflexes, which can be measured at the same rate as the speed of sound. However, they are unable to maintain this speed by running long distances, but are able to use this by jumping heights equivalent to four story buildings.

This species' lifespan is one of the longest in the supernatural world, up to 500 years old. It was told when interviewing one European Vampire subject that there was a member of his species surpassing his 600th birthday, although our investigators were unable to contact, meet and examine this individual. It was explained that he was able to obtain his great age from successfully hunting to prolong his strength and regenerative ability. However, if a European Vampire cannot feed on fresh blood at least once a week, then their metabolic system, strength and life expectancy fails.

They also have an excellent sense of smell. This species can smell a Werewolf within a 100 km radius and track it with a 99.9% success rate. They advise it is by the potent pheromones the Werewolf releases. Although European Vampires are severely allergic to silver, they often use silver coated weapons when hunting their favoured source of nourishment.

European Vampires appear to exist precariously on a double-edged sword, as their supernatural state can bring many benefits but just as many downfalls. As their bodies enter a form of biological stasis, they do not age and can maintain the same appearance for all of their existence. To some, this can be a vain benefit; however, the medical repercussions are plentiful. As mentioned previously, Vampires do breathe and they have a heartbeat which in turn moves the blood around their bodies to ensure motor function. However, from the almost suspended state their bodies exist in, their heart beat dramatically decreases, which means European Vampires encounter difficulty with strenuous physical activity. On this note, this species is required to spend a significant portion of their time slumbering to conserve their energy.

The idea of Vampires turning to dust from a stake to the heart; may be attributed to a European Vampire's rapid decomposition when it can be clinically called dead. As their bodies were partially shut down from the moment they were turned, their rate of decay is rapid with a drying effect. Even their skeletons are broken down to basic components in minimal time with only a biological 'ash' left. The full rate of decomposition occurs in seven days, which means an autopsy on this species must happen immediately from the time of death. This was noted when SSIT attempted to study a decapitated body. This mode of murder was a common one, to ensure the Vampire could not regenerate by imbibing blood.

~History~

The history of the European Vampire is long and they can be found in ancient texts spanning across several European and Middle Eastern countries. Tales of gods, demons and monsters who drank blood, creep out of ancient mythology and into local lore today. The bloodlust then as it does now, comes in differing shapes and sizes by its feeding and/or hunting pattern. Logically speaking, it's not surprising to see how European Vampires have evolved just as humans have, since they are a life form too, albeit a supernatural one.

The medieval ages and then the Witch Hunts witnessed two of the greatest upheavals for European Vampires. This parasitic hunter commonly preyed upon the rich to pay their way through the ages. Not only did hunting the wealthy fill their purses; however, the rich were considered safer to drink, with greater hygiene and less sickness than the poorer classes. But during the unrest, European Vampires had to hide their supernatural profiles to avoid being destroyed by religious authorities.

During the medieval times in the mountainous areas of Eastern Europe, there were many battles with European Werewolves. The wars were caused from the Vampires hunting the Werewolves to excess, with the volatile beasts rebelling. The battles became so public that it caught the attention of both the Roman and the Orthodox Churches, who were the predominant authorities. As the number of human victims caught in the crossfire continued to grow, church-empowered Knights, Sheriffs and other Noblemen became involved. Since there were too many witnesses, the Vampires slipped into secrecy and continued to hunt on the sly.

It was during the Witch Hunts that European Vampires began to prey upon humans with ESP. At first they were entranced by their auras which were caused by their different bio-electromagnetic fields. However, as soon as Vampires learned that the humans had telepathic, telekinetic, pyrokinetic gifts or who could 'see' into the past or future; they were put on the menu. Not only did Witches have to hide from Church Inquisitors, they also had to defend themselves against Vampires who mercilessly hunted them. The Witches then created protective 'spell bags' made from silver charms, garlic and 'Wolf's Bane' to keep the predators away, which also ended up keeping the wolves at bay. Werewolves are not allergic to garlic but 'Wolf's Bane' can make them ill, and then there is their severe allergy to silver.

By feeding on those with ESP, European Vampires were able to absorb many of their psychic abilities. Symbiogenesis theory is applied to microscopic organisms which imbibe other cells through ingestion which then becomes part of the larger cell's working machinery (5). Normally this isn't seen in animals as large as mammals, but Vampires are an example of this behaviour. It's conjectured that this is how the fable of Vampires charming their victims eventuated. By adapting their new psychic prowess to their hunting pattern, they were able to seduce their victims into either being led back to the European Vampire's coven to be fed on; or hypnotize them into blindly following their will for other purposes.

~Reproduction/Mating Habits~

European Vampires cannot reproduce by sexual means due to the fact that their reproductive organs are shut down during the transformation into Vampire. Sperm production in males ceases as do the ovaries in a female; therefore this species reproduce by infecting others with their blood.

When a European Vampire changes a human, the transformation can take anywhere between 1 - 7 days, depending on the amount of Vampire blood that was transferred. If the change was done deliberately, the transformation usually takes 24 hours and the new need to feed on blood is immediate once completed.

However, there have been instances in the past where a human may inadvertently be turned into a European Vampire by accidental contamination. This can occur if Vampire blood infects a cut or another injury on the human, similar to contamination by HIV. When this happens, the transformation can take up to 7 days, with the mutation a slow and painful process. With this example, often the human may not realize until it's too late and the majority of their bodily functions have been either necrotized or transformed.

On this note, when the European Vampire or its' coven discover what's happened, usually the accidental Vampire is destroyed. This species are exceptionally choosy whom they change due to the fact that they don't live alone. When a European Vampire transforms a human, it's to create a companion in their usually youthful form. A candidate is chosen by appearance, intelligence, wealth or other attributes. Then they are inducted where in most instances it could be the entire coven which share blood to transform them.

SOUTH AMERICAN VAMPIRE

~Physical Characteristics~

When a South American Vampire changes from human to other, their eyes turn completely red with their black pupils disappearing. All of their teeth become pointed and sharp and look similar to a piranha. This species of Vampire does not produce venom, however they rely on their teeth, nails and speed. The nails on the South American Vampire's hands become long and sharp like small knives and are the strongest nails of all the species SSIT encountered.

The strength of a South American Vampire is ten times that of a human. Like their European cousins, they have supernaturally fast reflexes, which can be measured at the same rate as the speed of sound. However, South American Vampires are able to maintain this speed by running long distances, but they cannot jump the same heights a European Vampire can.

This species longevity may reach 400 years if they are successful in hunting. If they cannot feed on fresh blood at least once every 5 days, then their metabolic system, strength and life expectancy fails. Using their ability to take extremely long breaths, they can successfully hunt underwater. By utilizing their multiple sharp teeth, they aren't averse to masticating the flesh of their victims to squeeze out more blood. It is because of this that many humans who are dragged from rivers such as the Amazon, are accounted to have been the victims of a piranha attack instead.

South American Vampires are extremely sensitive to the cold, and are the most susceptible to frost bite. Only once did SSIT hear of an instance where three South American Vampires ventured into a cold habitat, when they came to hunt the Lokoti Werewolves in Alaska. It was said this occurred during the summer, with the long hours of daylight which warmed temperatures. Instead, this species prefer the hot jungles or other regions where it does not snow, in South America.

On this note, it's not uncommon to find South American Vampires in Mexico either. Those who reside in this country often prey upon animals to avoid detection and therefore destruction by humans. Domestic live stock, such as goats are chosen for their accessibility and then the El Chupacabra aka 'the Mexican Goat Sucker', is blamed instead.

~History~

With the invasion and subsequent destruction of the Aztecs, Mayan, Incan and other South American cultures by the Spanish Conquistadores; it is difficult to trace the history of the South American Vampire past this period. Therefore, SSIT could not create an accurate timeline, tracking the evolution or distribution of this supernatural creature before the 15th Century. Therefore, the history of this species will begin at the end of the Aztec reign.

What happened to the Aztecs by the Spanish Conquistadores is a horrific chapter of history. Coupled with stories of how the Aztecs lived, fought and performed their religious ceremonies; the bloodied tales unsurprisingly lead us towards the South American Vampire's feeding pattern. A common practice of the Aztecs was to maim their opponent in battle, capture them and later use them in rituals. Aztec Priests would cut open the human sacrifices and pull out their organs, which would become apart of the ceremony and even, part of the ceremonial costume such as wearing the intestines around the neck (6). With this practice, it's little wonder that some of these Priests were South American Vampires.

After the decimation of the Aztecs, three South American Vampires migrated north. SSIT was told by local historians that when the Spanish put an end to the human sacrificial ceremonies, the three Aztec Priests decided to depart for new hunting grounds. The small coven travelled up through the United States, feeding on several Native American Tribes along the way, before reaching Canada where they heard of the Lokoti Werewolves.

The coven hunted for the Lokoti Tribe in the vast Alaska Range. The Tribal Elders shared their oral history with SSIT of when the South American Vampires attacked. It was a bloody battle with high casualties, with the South American Vampires ultimately destroyed by the stronger Lokoti Werewolves. However, the coven managed to kill several humans and members of the pack with their greater speed and knife-like nails, before they met their demise.

During the Spanish invasion, this species retreated from the cities to hide and hunt in the jungles or remote areas. By slipping into obscurity, they were able to continue to feed on human, albeit in significantly lesser numbers. Today, local authorities continue to account the victims as dying in 'animal attacks'. However, local Shaman in the smaller towns, pass on the history of the South American Vampire to younger generations in an effort to warn them.

~Reproduction/Mating Habits~

South American Vampires cannot sexually reproduce but instead create more of their kind by sharing their blood with the chosen.

If there's an accidental turning of a human who becomes infected, then the new Vampire is destroyed. This species are territorial and either lives alone or in small covens up to three Vampires but no more, as they do not like to share their hunting grounds. They prefer not to mingle with other covens like European Vampires do, and disagreements are 'settled' using their teeth and nails.

Whereas European Vampires prefer to live in towns and cities, South American Vampires are the exact opposite. They are by no means treated as 'the poor relation' but instead they receive the treatment of 'steer clear'. They may not be seen as 'refined' as their European cousins since they prefer the outdoors to hunt, they're not interested in intellect, nor are they choosy over who they feed on. However, they are extremely selective on whom they turn, and it's not uncommon for their kind to become dissatisfied with a new Vampire and killing/feeding on them instead.

NORTH AMERICAN VAMPIRE

~Physical Characteristics~

WARNING – This species of Vampire has poisonous fangs which can paralyse humans.

When they change from human to Vampire, their eyes glow and appear red on the outside of their irises, with yellow in the middle. Also, their foreheads become pronounced giving this species along with their glowing reddish eyes, a more 'demonic' appearance. Their upper canine teeth become long and sharp like the fangs on a snake. The venom is secreted by the fangs, which can paralyse humans for up to 3 days – if they survive an attack. The nails on the Vampire's hands become longer and sharper.

The strength of a North American Vampire is fifteen times that of a human and they are the strongest of the species investigated by SSIT. They have lightening fast reflexes, although they are not as fast as European or South American Vampires. They can run up to speeds of 360 km/h in short bursts and cannot jump as high as their European 'cousins'.

Their longevity is 300 years and it's believed their life span is shorter than the other species because of their faster metabolic rate, which attributes to their greater strength. South American Vampires need to hunt every third day to survive. However, after drinking from another Vampire or a Werewolf, 7 days can pass before they have to hunt again. It's not uncommon that this species will hunt their own kind, or cannibalize their own coven.

North American Vampires can perform strenuous physical activity with ease. With their bloodlust, they relish killing their victims in as a violent way as possible. Unlike the European variety that use cunning and covert tactics when hunting; they prefer a 'smash and grab' approach. Often, news reports of highway car-jacking with the vehicles destroyed and the owners missing can be attributed to their destructive nature.

~History~

The North American Vampire is an excellent example how polymorphic Vampire DNA can be; as this species is the result of a cross-contamination between the European and South American Vampire. This mongrel owes its history as well as its physical characteristics to its genetic 'forefathers'. But due to their nomadic culture, it's hard to pinpoint exactly how this genetic transference took place.

What SSIT has been able to conclude though, is this species did not exist prior to the 15th Century. With the advent of Christopher Columbus 'discovering' America and the subsequent invasion by European settlers, amidst this cross-cultural foray, was a coven of European Vampires. It's believed they came to the 'new world' to find fresh hunting grounds. Sometime during this period, their blood was mixed with a South American Vampire's, which incubated in a human and henceforth created the first North American Vampire.

Using elements of human history, as well as information obtained from an interview with a European Vampire; SSIT attempted to make a juxtaposition how this cross-contamination occurred.

The coven of European Vampires settled in the state which is now called Texas. Then, parts of this land were laid claim upon by Mexico. The territorial South American Vampires, who lived there, would have seen this geography as their hunting grounds. The South American Vampires would have fought the European Vampires and in this violent altercation, an unlucky human witness was pulled into the battle. The subsequent contamination by both Vampires occurred during the bloodshed.

To reconfirm, this is only conjecture however, several facts lend credence to this theory. Firstly, was the interview with the European Vampire subject who confirmed the story of a coven which departed for the 'Colonies', but only two survivors came back. They were granted sanctuary on their return because they sold an important piece of information; the existence of South American Vampires. With this knowledge, the 'Colonies' which eventually became the United States of America, was avoided by the European covens for over two centuries. It was not until the borders defining California, Texas and Mexico developed that European Vampires came to this country again.

When they did, they were shocked to discover the existence of the North American Vampire. Then to their horror, their refined sense of smell confirmed it was part of their DNA which had created them. Several European Vampire covens attempted to wipe out the 'accidental vampire'; however, with the North American Vampire's strength, the annihilation was unsuccessful.

~Reproduction/Mating Habits~

North American Vampires reproduce by sharing their blood with the chosen. However, they are the most violent of all of the species and prefer to hunt using brute force alone. Because of this, they are predominantly a male culture with very few covens containing a female.

When their kind attacks a woman, it's not in sexual assault as their sexual organs are no longer functioning. However, male North American Vampires derive sadistic pleasure from brutalizing their weaker victims. With this said, they often conflict with European Vampires where females are treated as equals, since their abilities match their male counterparts. If a male North American Vampire should try to feed on a female European Vampire; her coven will declare war and the majority of these battles are won by the Europeans due to their greater cunning, speed and use of silver swords.

Since North American Vampires are disorganized in their attacks, it's a frequent occurrence their human victims accidentally turn into more of their kind. When this happens, the new Vampire may begin a coven of their own. On a sadder note, there are other cases where the new Vampire may be so repelled by the experience, or if their loved ones were slaughtered; that they decide against becoming the monsters that made them. Then they painfully ignore their new bloodlust and starve to death after only three days.

WEST AFRICAN VAMPIRE

~Physical Characteristics~

As mentioned in the Introduction, most Vampires appear human but change form when fighting or feeding. However, there are a few species which may only attain a human appearance by feeding on this mammal. The West African Vampire is an example of this.

They are biologically a 'blank slate', that is to say they have a rare mutation of the albino gene, which has no skin pigmentation, hair or eye colouring. They literally are a translucent white because their bodies are missing the basic hormones which regulate their colouring. They have the unnerving appearance of a native to the continent of Africa, but with white afro hair, white eyes with small black pupils and a white, sometimes translucent skin.

This species is always male and as such, their feeding is concentrated on human males. The West African Vampire's choice of meal is not born from luxury; rather it is out of necessity. Not only do they drink the blood of the victim, but they take other fluids from the human body including from the pituitary gland. By ingesting the victim's blood, hormones and other bodily fluids, the West African Vampire adopts the colouring of its victim and sometimes other physical characteristics. This species is the most like a Shape Shifter, as its appearance can alter depending on the appearance of its meal.

On this note, West African Vampires choose human males to feed on because if it fed on a female and imbibed a large amount of oestrogen; it would greatly effect its shift in shape. Although SSIT cannot confirm if this could actually cause the male West African Vampire to change into a female, scientifically we can project it would be worse than a transsexual undergoing medical treatment to change gender.

West African Vampires do not have fangs or sharp elongated teeth, and its strength is five times that of a human being. Instead, this species uses the flora or fauna in its native area, such as specific plants or venom that has a paralysing effect, to make poisoned darts and stun their victims. When their prey has been neutralized, the West African Vampire then carries the human male to their hide-out/home to slowly drain them. The feeding is a drawn out process as they use many of the victim's bodily fluids to replenish its own. This is while the human is alive, paralysed and in subsequent agony throughout the entire time.

Their longevity is one of the shortest of the Vampire species, reaching 200 years old. Of course, this age can only be reached from successfully hunting to prolong its strength and regeneration. However, if a West African Vampire cannot feed at least once a month, then their metabolic system, strength and life expectancy fails.

~History~

One of the parts of the human body that the West African Vampire feeds on is the pituitary gland, which is responsible for growth hormones, prolactins and melanotrophins (7) to name a few. Since this is located in the brain, West African Vampires use tools such as straws carved out of wood or metal, to reach the gland. Because of this, they are often mistaken for another brain-feeding supernatural creature - the Zombie.

SSIT was investigating legends of the Zombie in Africa when we accidentally stumbled upon this unique species of Vampire. At first there were arguments within SSIT if this creature was in fact a Vampire, because its feeding was not just to exist on blood, but other bodily fluids. Also it could do something no other Vampire in the world can; it can procreate via sexual means. With these facts standing out, we postulated if the being was a Vampire? Or was it another kind of Shape Shifter? Or was it a new category of Zombie?

Some kinds of Zombie eat brain matter for the unique combination of chemicals and high concentrations of glucose. After further studying the West African Vampire, it became apparent it did not eat the brain matter but drank from one part of the brain; the pituitary gland. As Elisha Worthall continued to secretly observe this species, she noted a pattern. The colouring of the West African Vampire changed the more it fed, from white to dark.

After our subject fed on an obese human male, Elisha Worthall noted that its physical form was heavier. This lasted for approximately one month before the creature had to feed again. After drinking its' next victim and absorbing their blood and other bodily fluids, its skin colouring and weight changed again. It became obvious that we were dealing with a Shape Shifter and not a Zombie. Once we confirmed this Shape Shifter's longevity relied on this feeding pattern, we officially categorized the life form as the West African Vampire.

This species has an undistinguished past, as it relies on living quietly in society to hide its supernatural status. Should their Vampiric nature be discovered, then it could cost their lives when their feeding is disrupted. In the past of living in huts in villages to today of houses in the suburbs; this species has mastered the role of the 'inconspicuous neighbour'. They are permanently situated on the western side of the continent and use their natural habitat to their advantage. They would not consider leaving the geography which provides them with the tools they need, because if they miss a monthly meal; they are threatened with not just starvation but by their unusual white colour returning. This would attract unwanted attention and make hunting much more difficult.

~Reproduction/Mating Habits~

West African Vampires lead double lives as outwardly they can appear completely normal. They can consume food, preferably in soup form, and they can marry and procreate with a human female. When they reproduce, they create one child which is always a son. Upon reaching puberty, the sons learn how to hunt from their father. In most cases, the wives are oblivious to their husbands and sons' supernatural status. However, should the wife find out and threaten exposure, she is eliminated.

When the son 'turns' during adolescence, their colouring begins to fade and illnesses such as blood disorders set in. To stop their skin, hair and eye colour from turning albino, the father takes the son hunting as soon as possible. The older West African Vampire trains the younger in an eating pattern they will need to sustain for the rest of its existence. During puberty, the child also learns how to hide their new dietary requirements from society.

Scientifically, you could relate the West African Vampire's inability to sustain natural colouring or bodily functions, to the other species' necrotized flesh or organs. Just as another Vampire encounters difficulty with sunburn, so does this species with their albino colouring. Whereas the other species drink blood to heal the damaged skin cells, the West African Vampire imbibes the hormones necessary to darken their skin to provide better protection. However, their kind like all the species profiled in this report, rely on the humans they consume to function in their day-to-day lives.

CONCLUSION

The West African Vampire was the most interesting species SSIT examined. They appear to embody not just Vampiric tendencies, but also incorporate elements of other supernatural creatures. This life form shares similarities with not only Zombies but with Egyptian Mummies.

When examining objectively the process of Mummification, this ritual can be seen as a human's attempt at longer life. Vampire bodies exist in a semi-stasis, which is the result of the necrotizing of the flesh or other organs. The Ancient Egyptian mummification process entails several of the deceased's organs such as the brain and heart, to be extracted as the body is dried with salt, to preserve the flesh. The extracted organs are not discarded but are kept close to the Mummy in Canopic jars, so the dead may use them in the 'After Life' (8).

One could speculate that the embalming ritual was the Ancient Egyptian's primitive attempt at Vampirism; the flesh is preserved with the no longer functioning organs removed. Depicted in Hollywood movies, it is the Mummy itself enacting the horrible deeds of taking the organs from the living to replace its own, so it may live once more. Although this is clearly fiction, it's remarkable how these relate to the West African Vampire. This species feeds not only on blood, but it also takes fluids from other parts of the body.

The Ancient Egyptian curse entails that if a tomb robber or archaeologist (which sometimes can be one and the same) unearths a Mummy or their burial treasure; certain death can come to the disturber. Historically, it is also interesting to note the run of 'bad luck' which has fallen on different members of archaeological digs. For example, the infamous unearthing of Tutankhamen.

One may argue that it was a set of circumstances which when lumped together, is simply called coincidence. But all of the cases that SSIT have investigated on supernatural topics such as phantom lights, haunted houses, Ley Lines, Stone Circles, ESP as well as the Bermuda Triangle; what's proven is sometimes a series of natural events combine to create a supernatural event. Aside from the stories of misfortune on the Tutankhamen dig, it's interesting to note that many Egyptians show a sizeable respect in leaving the ancients to rest in peace; which is the same wariness as Koreans may feel towards the mine fields that separate the North and South of their countries. Why tempt fate which may seal your own?

The cross-cultural similarities between Vampirism and other facets of the supernatural are so alike that the borders between them can be blurred. When one looks in hindsight at the fact European Vampires are not the strongest in the supernatural world, so their hunting pattern is traditionally nocturnal. This is not just for the fact that their skin has difficulty healing from sunburn, but because their food source aka humans, are usually slumbering during night-time. European Vampires use their agility by slipping unseen into the bedrooms, which saves the Vampire from physical exertion if they hunted them when they were awake. If the Vampire was unlucky, their feeding may be interrupted by another human walking in. The witness finds the Vampire lying on top so it will have a better angle to place their mouths on the jugular and hence; they're thought to be the Incubus or Succubus who are also called sex demons.

The different kinds of Asian Vampire also prefer to hunt at night. Since there were several subdivisions of this species, SSIT could not include them all in this report. Instead, we launched a separate investigation into this group. Just as Asia is divided into many cultural entities and languages, so too were its Vampires. To briefly mention, a common characteristic of some subspecies, was a hunting pattern which made them similar to the West African Vampire. Whereas the West African Vampire is all-male and hunted male-kind; many subspecies of Asian Vampires were all-female and hunted female-kind, including pregnant women or newborns.

Whilst we can analyse a Vampire's physiology and why it takes from others, the explanation of how Vampire DNA was first created, still eludes us. What caused this biological enigma on a world wide scale? How did the bloodlust develop in creatures whose supernatural longevity depends on the natural world? As a Vampire Bat must drink ten times its weight to survive; its paranormal cousins follow similar behaviour and feed on human.

~~~~~~~~~~~~~~~~~~~~~~~~~~~~~~~~~~~~

SSIT Report on Human/Animal Shape Shifters

INTRODUCTION

The Supernatural Scientific Investigative Team found Human/Animal Shape Shifters to be the most intriguing facet of the vast Shape Shifter family. This paranormal creature has ties to both the natural and supernatural, in history, physique and ability. Whilst Werewolves have a prehistoric 'forefather' and the exact beginnings of the Vampire remain in a fog of speculation; the Human/Animal Shape Shifter timeline runs parallel with human development.

All across the globe, there are clans/families of humans who can turn into an animal of similar size which is native to their geography. The Human/Animal Shape Shifter can turn into one animal only, not a variety, and the animal it turns into is genetically predetermined. For example, if a child is born to a Shifter parent who morphs into a lion; so will they. The ability to transform from human to animal and back again starts from birth.

However, the cause of turning into the particular animal can differentiate. Depending on the clan and/or family, each has a story of how the first transformation took place, but can be based on one of three ways; from spirit possession to genetic mutation and even through cross-species reproduction. Although Human/Animal Shape Shifters are varied; e.g., tigers in South and South East Asia, panthers in South America, rhinoceros in Africa or polar bears in the Arctic; they all share a common trait. When in animal form, their eyes appear completely black with no irises or whites showing.

When shifting to animal form, their black pupils dilute to encompass the entire front of the eyeball. Their human sight switches to a transcendental vision which is something else. The Human/Animal Shape Shifter subject we interviewed quoted, "our sight switches from clear lines of shapes and solids, to weird, quasi, energy fields. We don't see the shape of a tree or its leaves, but we see the energy coming up from the ground and stretching out to the branches." This field of vision extends not only to flora or fauna, but to the very earth itself.

In the beginnings of SSIT at Cambridge University, we ran an investigation on Ley Lines. Using a 25th Century scanning device, Elisha Worthall was able to confirm previously established Ley Lines as well as detect several more. Ley Lines connected many of the Stone Circles situated in the UK, with others branching across the globe in a worldwide network. What was discussed in the SSIT Report on Reincarnation, the Circulate Mainframe has surface maps which profiles Earth's major Ley Lines. Some scientists have likened Earth as a major super conductor, being bombarded with energy from the sun and the planet itself generating electrical storms in its atmosphere. The Ley Lines conduct this charge although there is the occasional disruption. There are humans such as psychics and those with ESP which are able to sense Ley Lines and other places of power, and SSIT discovered with this report that Human/Animal Shape Shifters are another who can, too.

Through a highly evolved sense of survival, Shifters have displayed many uncanny talents. One, is their unique sight in seeing the energy fields of their environment including Ley Lines. Two, is a finely honed sense of smell, which can pick up the most minuscule change in the atmosphere. In the past, there have been recorded instances where marine life or even some land-based animals, run for safety hours before a tsunami hits. Or, animals in volcanically active areas may vacate their homelands days before an eruption. Human/Animal Shape Shifters share this ability and use it to keep their clans/families safe. Thirdly, is the behaviour some animals display around humans, such as dogs reacting badly to a visitor in their territory. Then the seemingly nice person exhibits dangerous tendencies and the saying arises, "animals sense these things." This can also be said with Shifters, whose similar instincts help them avoid unsafe situations.

Other physical attributes shared by Human/Animal Shape Shifters is their muscle. Most of their kind displays strength, which is fifty times that of a human, but it can also depend on the kind of animal it shifts into. For example, a Shifter which morphs into a rhinoceros is stronger than one that changes into a panther. All have regenerative capabilities, which may not be as powerful as a European Werewolf, but faster than a human. However, like their Werewolf and Vampire 'cousins', Human/Animal Shape Shifters are severely allergic to silver. Any kind of contact with this metal can result in serious injury. They can be as strong as a Lokoti Werewolf, but Shifters do not have supernatural speed. When they change into their animal form, they match the same speed of the animal.

Although this paranormal creature is related to the Vampire and Werewolf by a similar cellular structure, which transforms them from human to other; a major difference with Human/Animal Shape Shifters, is they do not have the bloodlust. Their kind does not depend on blood or flesh to maintain its health or longevity, which is similar to a human's lifespan. In fact, if the Shifter morphs into an animal which is a herbivore, in human form they will carry on a vegetarian diet. But like the breeds of Werewolf, the impact of a full moon affects their brain chemistry and triggers them to change although they can also revert between cycles.

When our Investigators pointed out this similarity with the differing breeds, the interview subject became offended. We were advised that Shifters are the deadly enemies of both Werewolves and Vampires and will attempt to destroy them upon sight. This is because Human/Animal Shape Shifters are preyed upon by both, especially by the Vampire. Since the species prey upon Werewolves for their strength and regenerative capabilities, when a Werewolf couldn't be found, SSIT learned that Vampires would hunt Shifters instead. Elisha Worthall then tried to persuade the subject that Lokoti Werewolves, whom had become her friends, were not man-eaters. However, their alternate food source of fresh kill from the animal kingdom, did not placate the Shifter who turns into a member of this realm.

Indeed, the Human/Animal Shape Shifter advised SSIT very adamantly that his kind were not cannibals. That is to say, even Shifters who turned into tigers or other predators have never consumed another Shifter, not even in animal form. Shifters abhor Werewolves for being unable to control their bloodlust and they detest Vampires for their unrelenting thirst. Both are blamed for entire families/clans disappearances and numbers are still dropping. It is for this reason that as soon as a Shifter reaches sexual maturity, they will mate in an effort to ensure their family's and/or clan's future.

When this paranormal creature mates with a human, the foetus develops as a Human/Animal Shape Shifter. They are monogamous although they do have a powerful sex drive, which impels them to reproduce. They will pick a partner based on fertility and if they detect a human is infertile, they will not initiate a sexual relationship. When searching for a reproductive partner, Shifters release a potent pheromone to lure in a perspective mate. During sexual intercourse, the pheromones also act as an aphrodisiac to encourage conception. However, after several interviews with a Shifter and one including his mate, SSIT discovered another aspect to this. Not only does the scent heighten desire and enhance sexual gratification, but it has an addictive side affect to bind the human to the creature.

This means if they are parted for more than 24 hours, the human will go through withdrawal. The symptoms can be likened to what an alcoholic or drug addict may go through in rehabilitation; shaking, sweating, vomiting, heart palpations, sleeplessness, headaches or even hallucinations. However, like recovering from an addiction, the physical sensations do decrease in time. SSIT was advised of this by a human widow who lost her Shifter mate in a European Vampire attack, and suffered withdrawal during her mourning.

Like the breeds of Werewolf, there has never been a case of differing Human/Animal Shape Shifters mating with each other. For example, a person who can turn into a rhinoceros will not attempt to mate with a person who can turn into a tiger. Just as their powerful sex drives urge them to find a fertile partner; it also deters them from cross-contamination and creating a rhino-tiger. When the clans were larger, it was encouraged for two Shifters who turned into the same animal to mate. But with the decrease in population, their kind had no choice but to propagate with humans. In doing so, their pheromones ensure devotion in the human, instead of fear or repulsion.

The subject of sexual reproduction is in fact tied to the Human/Animal Shape Shifter past, just as it's connected to their future. In the very beginning when primitives painted in caves or carved pictures on temples, Shifters have courted humanity. In

Egypt, there are pictures of gods with human bodies but with animal heads, such as Anubis, the God of the Dead, and his features of a jackal. Or, in one of the creation myths, the human-like sun god Re, hatched from the egg of a goose called the Great Cackler (9). In Greek legend there was a Minotaur, part man and part bull. Also in Greek mythology there is the story of the young woman Leda, who was seduced by Zeus who came to her in the form of a swan. Attached to this story, is another that Leda produced two eggs which contained her children, including the famous beauty, Helen of Troy (10).

There are legends from all over the globe, about gods or creatures who could switch from animal to human or be both at once. In Celtic mythology there is Morrigan, the Goddess of War, who turns into a crow to feed on the fallen in battle (11). In Northern Europe, there is the trickster Loki, who could transform into several animals, including birds (12). In the Arctic, there's Yup'ik and Inupiaq legends of a Raven Man who could switch from animal to human, took a human wife and then their sons also turned into ravens at will (13). In North American mythology, there are tricksters who take the shape of ravens or other animals native to that geography and their dealings with the fairer sex (14). Then in South America particularly the Andean region, there is artwork of fanged half human and half animal creatures as well as jaguars or pumas (15). In India there are the avatars of Vishnu (16) and in Korea with the Myth of Tan'Gun, a tiger and a bear begged Hwanung to turn them into humans, with the bear eventually being given a woman's body (17).

Moving away from ancient times and through to the present day; SSIT came across numerous relationships formed between humans with ESP and Human/Animal Shape Shifters. There are dozens of stories of Medicine Men, Shamans, Druids, Witches or Wizards who imbibe potions or other plant substances, to embark on hallucinogenic journeys. Often on these 'voyages', they would think they could turn into a particular animal or 'become one' with them. Just as the psychics would feel an affinity to an animal, they would also protect Shifters who could turn into them. Another commonality they share is the connection to the earth, with both Seers and Shifters drawn to Ley Lines. Just as Human/Animal Shape Shifters can see the energy in their surroundings, they have informed SSIT they can differentiate psychics by their greater energy fields, too. This in turn, made the Shifter protective of the human, as well as attractive as a suitable mate.

During the Witch Hunts, several clans of Shifters and psychics from differing countries, banded together to form the Conclave. In secret meeting places around Europe, the Mediterranean, the Americas or Asia, which were near power-based landmarks, Seers and Shifters would help each other. Not only did they have to contend with Werewolves or Vampires preying upon them, but humans as well. Murderous religious figures from the dominating churches, vied for their extermination in similar ways, which incriminates Hitler and the Nazis today. Shifters whom had protected humans by fighting off Werewolves or Vampires in their territory, or Seers who treated humans as Healers and Midwives, found themselves hunted by the very people they had helped in the past.

It is for this reason that the Conclave remains a secret from society. Only my investigative partner Elisha Worthall, was permitted to attend a meeting, being a Circulator. Both Shifters and psychics can see a Circulator's aura, which is caused by their bio-electromagnetic fields being in temporal flux. Although the Conclave was open to learning about the other secret society called the Circulate, when Elisha Worthall offered to introduce them to the Lokoti Werewolf pack, it was met with mistrust and refusal. Indeed, she was made to swear never to tell the Lokoti Tribe about the Conclave and to my understanding, she never has. Although SSIT has shared our reports on the Different Breeds of Werewolf and the Separate Species of Vampires with the Lokoti, this report like the Conclave's existence, will remain hidden.

LATIN AMERICAN BLACK PANTHER/HUMAN SHAPE SHIFTER

~Physical Characteristics~

To begin with, Black Panthers are in fact either jaguars, leopards, cougars or other large species of cat; whose coats look black by a melanistic colour variant. This rarity is caused by an excessive black pigment called melanin (18). The Latin American Black

Panther/Human Animal Shape Shifter is a black jaguar whose natural habitat is South America.

In the natural world, jaguars are a compact and muscled animal and can be up to 76 cm's tall from the shoulders down and weigh up to 160 kg's. Being short and stocky, they can crawl, climb, swim and when hunting, they prefer to stalk and ambush their prey. They have extremely strong jaws and favour biting down on the head and delivering death by its teeth piercing the skull. In the wild, they are a solitary animal who only meet to court and mate, with a male's territory incorporating two or three females (19).

In the supernatural world, Latin American Black Panther/Human Animal Shape Shifters are distinguishable by their slightly larger size and having black eyes instead of golden ones. They look almost completely black, which works in their favour if they should hunt at night. They are just as deft at climbing and attacking as their natural cousins, though they are stronger. In both human and animal form, their strength is forty times that of a human.

When shifting into their jaguar shape, the black fur springs forth from the pores in the skin. However, when we examined this kind of Shifter in human form, SSIT noted that there appeared to be more pores in the skin than a normal human being. This would account for the thick coat rather than bald patches appearing on the animal.

Unlike the jaguars in the wild, when in animal form this Shifter will share its hunting grounds with its clan. In most cases, their human mate will remain home and the Shifter parent will hunt with its Shifter children and relatives. For the majority of the time, this will occur over the period of the full moon, however, it's not unusual to change between lunar cycles.

~History~

Although jaguars aren't typically found in the Andes (20), Latin American Black Panther/Human Animal Shape Shifters are an exception. SSIT uncovered a story linking this Shifter to the Inca culture. Apparently an Incan warrior found an injured Black Panther in the mountainous forest whilst hunting one day. Since jaguars and pumas are highly respected in a culture which worshiped cat-like spirits, the warrior carried the animal back to where he lived, in the famed city of Machu Picchu which today is called 'the cloud city' or 'the lost city' (21). Perched high on the mountain tops in Peru, this Incan city is shrouded in history and myth.

The warrior took the creature to the priests in the main temple, wondering if this rare animal was a sign from the Gods. The priests then cared for the animal, thinking something similar as it had been many years since a Black Panther had been sighted in their area. When the creature was strong again, it transformed into a young woman before the humans' eyes. She spoke to them in an old language they had difficulty understanding, which was a primitive dialect of Chimu. Eventually the priests came to understand that the girl/creature was looking for a powerful Seer from the Chimu people that the Inca had conquered.

The young woman told them that her clan of Shifters sought this Seer's counsel because they could smell that danger was on the horizon. The priests were told this Seer could not only see into the past or future, but travel to these eras as well. This intrigued the religious and political leaders of the city, and they sent Chaski (22) - running messengers - to other Incan cities such as Cuzco, to see if any sons of local leaders who were being educated in the Inca way, matched the woman's description.

As they waited for a reply, the young woman who was found attractive was sent to sleep in the building which housed the city's mamakuna. These were beautiful young women who were taken from their homes to weave cloth, brew chicha beer, engage in religious activities and were assigned to arranged marriages (23). However, the Shifter was not expected to weave or brew, as she could well have been a deity in the priests' eyes. Instead, she befriended a girl who made clothes for her, as well as helped her learn their language.

Since the Andean region is volcanically active, which also means earthquakes in the area (24), the Shifter soon proved her usefulness by sensing when a tremor would shake the city. She would also warn if there would be storms in the tempestuous area, using her finely tuned instincts. At first, the priests were wary of her hunting on a full moon in case she might run away, but the Black Panther would always return to the city and to her human form.

Machu Picchu was built in a sacred area to the Inca, which SSIT accounts today as being built on a Ley Line junction, which makes it a power-based landmark. A psychic priest knew this was what attracted the Shifter and why she protected the people by warning of natural disaster. However, the young woman had always told she couldn't remain, as she had to look for the powerful Seer.

Then one day a young man came to the city. He had been the son of a Chimu leader but was educated in Cuzco, in the Inca way (25). Instead of returning to his Inca-conquered lands, he went on a pilgrimage. The psychic priest and the Shifter were immediately entranced by the stranger's bright aura only they could see, and escorted him into the temple.

Over a banquet, he told stories of hunting with a tribe who from imbibing Yaje, "became one with the mother puma", and used the extra sensory perception bestowed by her. His stories and his aura fascinated them and he was asked to stay. However, the young man said he had to circulate a warning to the former Chimu and now Incan People, of a 'Conquering Storm' which would change their way of life forever.

The young man left that night to continue his quest and the next morning, they found that the Shifter was gone, too. Her friend in the mamakuna told the priests that she woke in the middle of the night to see a large Black Panther with black eyes sitting by her bed. The creature nodded its head towards the girl's shawl, indicating she should leave as well. Then the animal leapt out of the window and into the night and was never seen again. The psychic priest knew that the Shifter had gone to tell her Clan of the Seer's message and he thought it would be unwise if he left the warning unheeded.

Although this reads as a fable, interestingly there are several commonalities linking fiction to fact. This story is dated to the early 16th Century and the Spanish Conquistadores arrived in 1532 (26). The Inca way of life did change forever, as did the lives of so many South Americans. Although the Conquistadores never reached Machu Picchu when the 'Lost City' was discovered by the outside world from 1874 onwards (27), it was in ruins. Whereas we can only speculate if the city was vacated because of the warning, or where exactly they went, there is an intriguing clue. In 1995, the frozen remains of an Incan teenaged girl had been found near a summit in the Andes in southern Peru. She'd been murdered as a sacrifice to the gods and wrapped in fine cloth (28).

The young man with the aura was a Circulator and is in fact a friend of my partner in SSIT, Elisha Worthall. With Purto's help and using the 25th Century technology of the Circulate's Viewing Room, he was able to confirm that the young maiden had been the Shifter's friend, who'd been in the mamakuna. These women were used in religious ceremonies although human sacrifices weren't as common in the Inca as they were with the Aztecs. Perhaps the girl was killed to join her friend the Shifter, who the Inca thought had been a deity? Or maybe she was supposed to appease the gods who the Inca thought were responsible for causing earthquakes and bad weather, now that their warning system was gone. Then of course we ponder if the Shifter tried to warn the girl, her life was in danger before she left?

~Reproduction/Mating Habits~

Whereas jaguars in the wild have one male mating with two or three females in his territory, Latin American Black Panther/Human Animal Shape Shifter's are monogamous. They will choose their partner by how fertile they smell and the male Shifter will turn overprotective of the female they impregnate. Or, if a female Shifter is impregnated by a human, her potent pheromones will make the man devoted and protective of her. This is to aid the continuation of their species, whose numbers are reducing with each new generation.

This Shifter is born in human form, but transforms into cubs on a full moon. Their young are just as helpless as babies or cubs are, in the natural world. The latter are born blind and do not gain their sight until two weeks old (29), whereas human children can immediately see. Cubs are weaned at three months although they remain in the birth den for six months (30); similar to human infants who can be taken off the breast and put onto formula. Jaguars accompany their mothers on hunts for the first one to two years (31) whilst Shifter young hunt with either their Shifter mother or father, up to eighteen years.

Upon sexual maturity between the ages of eighteen to twenty, the former child will leave home to establish their own. They will actively seek a mate to begin reproducing as soon as possible. Their strong sex drives can interfere with their concentration and make them restless, similar to the effects the full moon has on their psyche. Once they find their reproductive partner, Shifters embody the very notion of 'settling down', with their raging hormones restabilizing.

CIRCULATE ADDENDUM:

This was all that was recovered of the SSIT Report on Human/Animal Shape Shifters from Dr. Xavier Bell's laptop computer. On his desktop however, we did find lab results from the various tissue samples and blood tests taken from consenting subjects. It's believed that this report would have physically profiled and given the histories of four different clans, until World War Three made further investigation impossible.

Sadly, Dr. Xavier Bell passed away soon afterwards at the age of 77 years. He is survived by his telepathic daughter, granddaughter and great granddaughter, Lady Yvette Worthall, Josephine Horley and Danika Riverclaw. The telepathy is attributed to his late wife Belle Dupont, whom he met during the SSIT Report on ESP and the subsequent Report on Reincarnation. His best friend and co-worker Elisha Worthall ensured that all the reports SSIT made were uploaded into the Circulate Mainframe for future posterity.

~~~~~~~~~~~~~~~~~~~~~~~~~~~~~~~~~~~~~~

AFTERWORD

The Circulate is a secret society of humans who can either calculate or circulate through time. The organization had 696 members, consisting two thirds of Calculators and one third of Circulators. Circulate Headquarters was situated inside of a habitation dome on Mars 250,000 years ago, when the planet had vegetation and an atmosphere. Although the base was situated in the past, it operated on 25th Century technology of crystallized circuitry and specialized light beams.

Upon evolving to the space time continuum, the Headquarters was destroyed to protect the secret of the Circulate's existence. This ensured that the habitation dome wouldn't be seen when mankind created telescopes. However, there is a backup Headquarters on Taurus Six, which is an exact replica of the Martian design. This is run by the Circulate Mainframe, which acts as Calculator to the Circulator Bianca Sabre. On Earth or more specifically, within a small tribe in the Alaska Range; she is known as the last 'Light Person', as well as the first female Lokoti Werewolf.

~~~~~~~~~~~~~~~~~~~~~~~~~~~~~~~~~~~~~~

FOOTNOTES

(1) Cotterell, Arthur. <u>The Encyclopedia of Mythology; Classical, Celtic, Norse</u>. Annes Publishing Limited. London. 1996. p. 226

(2) *ibid*, p. 226

(3) http://en.wikipedia.org/wiki/Vampire_watermelon

(4) http://en.wikipedia.org/wiki/Arnica_montana

(5) Bormanis, Andre. <u>Star Trek Science Logs</u>. Pocket Books. New York. 1998. p. 82

(6) Burchell, David. <u>Lecture Notes from History 1: The World Encircled 1450 - 1750</u>. Faculty of Humanities and Social Sciences. University of Western Sydney, Nepean Campus. 1996

(7) http://en.wikipedia.org/wiki/Pituitary_gland

(8) Chisholm, Jane and Millard, Anne and Jackson, Ian. <u>The Usborne Book Of The Ancient World.</u> The Usborne Publishing Ltd. London. 1991. p. 18

(9) *ibid*, p. 21

(10) Cotterell, <u>op.cit</u>, p. 57

(11) Cotterell, Arthur (Ed.) <u>World Mythology</u>. Paragon Books. Bath. 2000. p. 96

(12) *ibid*, p.120

(13) *ibid*, p.136

(14) *ibid*, p.268

(15) *ibid*, p.294

(16) *ibid*, p.149

(17) *ibid*, p.200

(18) http://en.wikipedia.org/wiki/Black_panther

(19) http://en.wikipedia.org/wiki/Jaguar

(20) *ibid*

(21) Wise, Karen. <u>Cloud Cities Of The Inka</u>. Weidenfeld & Nicolson. London. 1997

(22) *ibid*, p. 15

(23) *ibid*, p. 25

(24) Cotterell (Ed.), <u>op. cit</u>. p. 294

(25) Wise. <u>op.cit</u>. p. 20

(26) *ibid*, p. 2

(27) http://en.wikipedia.org/wiki/Machu_picchu

(28) Wise. <u>op.cit</u>. p. 32

(29) <u>op.cit</u>, http://en.wikipedia.org/wiki/Jaguar

(30) *ibid*

(31) *ibid*

FURTHER READING

Goldman, Jane. <u>The X-Files Book of Unexplained, Volume Two</u>. Simon & Schuster. London. 1996

Pennick, Nigel. <u>Mysteries of the Ancient World: Leylines</u>. Weidenfeld & Nicolson. London. 1997

Warren, Joshua P. <u>How to Hunt Ghosts: A Practical Guide</u>. Fireside. New York. 2003

About the Author

Elisha Worthall, Dr. Xavier Bell, the breeds of Werewolf, species of Vampire and kinds of Human/Animal Shape Shifters; are all fictitious characters in the sci-fi, paranormal romance novels called The Circulate Series by K.R. Smith. The SSIT Reports were written as an accompaniment and a contrast to the series, since the books can be 'mushy' in nature ;-) Being a geek at heart, the author loved researching science fact, which she hopes the reader enjoyed the 'shape shift' into science fiction.

Discover the eBooks by K.R. Smith published at Smashwords.com:

http://www.smashwords.com/profile/view/onaya3

Discover the paperbacks by K.R. Smith published at Lulu.com:

http://stores.lulu.com/onaya3

Connect with me online:

http://www.twitter.com/onaya3

http://www.facebook.com/Circulate.Series.KRSmith?ref=ts

~ The Circulate Series ~
By K.R. Smith

~ Book One: Circulate ~

Elisha Baker learns something new about herself when she attends the haunted international boarding school, Hamilton's College.

~ Book Two: Circulating ~

Elisha and her friends graduate from Hamilton's and the Circulate; to begin University and SSIT – Supernatural Scientific Investigative Team.

~ Book Three: Circulation ~

Armed with degrees, Elisha and her friends continue with SSIT. However adult life isn't as straightforward as they imagined, especially when an investigation into past lives interferes with a present romance.

~ Book Four: Progeny ~

Alexandrina and twin brother Bastian, grew up without a mother and a distant father. But it's to Jarrod's chagrin that his daughter mirrors his late wife, with the fact that she too is a Circulator.

~ Book Five: Ardor & Redolence ~

Arabella joins her grandmother on a SSIT case and meets Emanuel Riverclaw. Eventually they marry and create twins Julian and Jessica; a son who will become a Lokoti Werewolf like his father and a daughter who is a Circulator like her mother.

~ Book Six: Scent ~

At first the Last Circulator can't stand the tribe's most dangerous Werewolf, then Bianca and Declan's fiery arguments turn into something else.

~ Book Seven: Sororate ~

Claws come out in the marriage of the tribe's first female Lokoti Werewolf and the world's last European Werewolf; who spend their tumultuous years together traveling the world and through time.

~ Book Eight: Small Fry ~

Declan swore he wouldn't create anymore European Werewolves like himself, so his wife's new condition has his already hot blood boiling.

~ Book Nine: Alma ~

The new girl in Alma High School called Mali Roanne, suspects there's more than meets the eye with her Lokoti friends. However Mali is hiding a supernatural secret of her own.

~ Book Ten: Heterogeneous ~

In a space age, the different breeds of Werewolves are confined to Earth because of the influence of its one moon. But there's no such holds on the separate species of Vampires or even Human/ Animal Shape Shifters.

~ Book Eleven: Cohesion ~

Parents become grandparents when their children marry and procreate; with all of the different elements of the supernatural combining into one unusual family.

~ Book Twelve: Full Circle ~

The end is nigh, with answers as to why the futuristic Circulate technology never advanced past the 25th Century; because humankind doesn't.

www.ingramcontent.com/pod-product-compliance
Lightning Source LLC
Chambersburg PA
CBHW050905120626
46554CB00003B/1022